You c

If you

For Guy Brendan - M.R.

For Theo - L.L.

ORCHARD BOOKS

338 Euston Road, London NW1 3BH

Orchard Books Australia Level 17/207 Kent Street, Sydney, NSW 2000

First published in 2013 by Orchard Books

ISBN 978 1 40831 200 1

Text © Michelle Robinson 2013   Illustrations © Leonie Lord 2013

The rights of Michelle Robinson to be identified as the author and of Leonie Lord to be identified as the illustrator

of this book have been asserted by them in accordance with the Copyright, Designs and Patents Act, 1988.

A CIP catalogue record for this book is available from the British Library.

1 3 5 7 9 10 8 6 4 2

Printed in China

Orchard Books is a division of Hachette Children's Books,

an Hachette UK company.

www.hachette.co.uk

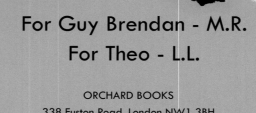

DING DONG GORILLA!

MICHELLE ROBINSON   LEONIE LORD

ORCHARD

You know we ordered a pizza?

A GREAT **BIG**

ONE WITH **EXTRA** CHEESE?

Well, I'm afraid I have some **BAD** news ...

YOU SEE, while you were upstairs, getting ready for dinner, the doorbell rang.

DING DONG!

I thought it must be the pizza boy, so I answered it.

DIAL A PIZZA

It was
DEFINITELY
NOT
the
PIZZA
BOY.

I didn't invite the gorilla in,
he just barged past me.

He went straight to my
TOY BOX
and tipped everything
out to get at *the*
CRAYONS.

He did LOTS of **COLOURING IN**, but he wasn't very good at staying between the lines.

But that's not the **BAD** NEWS...

When the gorilla got bored he **STOMPED OFF** to watch TV.

He went through all my movies,
but at least he put them
away afterwards.

JUST NOT IN THE RIGHT PLACES...

That's not the BAD news, either.

Next, the gorilla wanted to play dressing up.

I COULDN'T STOP HIM!

He put on all my clothes (and most of yours, too).

THEN
HE LEFT
THEM IN A
DIRTY HEAP
ON MY BEDROOM FLOOR.

I thought perhaps the gorilla was over-excited,
so I sent him outside to get some fresh air . . .

. . . but he got some fresh flowers instead.
The garden doesn't look so pretty anymore . . .

The gorilla wanted to play

FOOTBALL

next, but it was getting
a bit dark.

So we came
back inside.

It wasn't me
who broke the

VASE...

or the
WINDOW...

or the **chair**...

And that STILL
isn't the BAD news...

By now the gorilla was GETTING REALLY **HUNGRY**. I was a bit scared, but he wasn't interested in me.

He wanted to bake a **CHOCOLATE CAKE**.

Baking for Gorillas

HE HAD JUST TURNED ON THE BLENDER WHEN THE DOORBELL RANG AGAIN.

THIS TIME IT **REALLY** **WAS** the PIZZA BOY.

He looked
surprised to see us.

He ran away before
I could pay him.

I suppose that's quite

GOOD

news, really.

But the gorilla ran
away when he heard
you coming downstairs.

So you probably won't
believe that HE made
all this mess.

You are BOUND to
blame me and send
me to bed without
any pizza.